Elon, Musk, and Jeff

A Parody

By *Marshal Haze*

Introduction

This story is a whimsical and humorous tale set in a world where Elon Musk is the Emperor and Mark Zuckerberg is a world-class spy.

The story follows Mark's attempts to stop Emperor Elon's reign of laughter by doing things such as infiltrating a gala and engaging in a dance-off for the fate of the world. Along the journey joins none other than Jeff Bezos.

The story is filled with absurd scenarios, such as a roller coaster looping around the Eiffel Tower and a fleet of dancing Tesla cars. If you're in search of a good laugh, this story might be for you. Enjoy!

Elon, Mark, and Jeff: A Parody

Once upon a time, in a future reality on Earth that seemed straight out of a Saturday morning cartoon, the world was under the spell of none other than Elon Musk, who had crowned himself Emperor of the World. However, this wasn't your typical world domination scenario. Elon had undergone a peculiar transformation, adopting the flamboyant personality of King Julian from the movie Madagascar. He ruled with a zest for life, dance, and a seemingly never-ending quest for laughter.

Elon's journey to becoming Emperor of the World began when he transformed his SpaceX into "SpacePartyX." He declared that his mission was no longer to colonize Mars but to turn it into the universe's hottest dance floor, complete with zero-gravity raves and interstellar DJ sets. His first decree as Emperor was to rename the Red Planet "Party Planet."

To fund his global takeover, Elon created an array of eccentric corporations. "MarsMunchies" specialized in interplanetary snacks, with products like Martian marshmallow moons and asteroid apple pie.

"NeuraLinkieWinkie" was Elon's venture into mind-reading technology, which he used to organize surprise birthday parties for unsuspecting citizens.

Meanwhile, on the other side of the world, a secret organization known as "Guardians of Giggles" had taken notice of Elon's antics. Led by the enigmatic Mark Zuckerberg, the Guardians were a high-tech, well-funded group committed to defending the world from the laughter-induced tyranny of Elon. Their headquarters, disguised as a giant circus tent, was a hub of advanced gadgets and gags.

 Mark Zuckerberg was the world's top-secret agent and renowned for his impeccable timing and never-ending arsenal of whoopee cushions. Armed with the latest in laugh-suppressing technology, Mark set out to thwart Elon's grand plans.

The first encounter between Mark and Emperor Elon occurred at the "GigaGiggle Gala," an event where the entire world was invited to laugh along with their new ruler. Elon had built a roller coaster that looped around the Eiffel Tower, while a fleet of dancing Tesla cars performed a synchronized electric slide. The whole world was in stitches, and Mark knew he had to act fast.

Mark, disguised as a clown, infiltrated the gala. He had an elaborate plan involving a giant rubber chicken and a whoopee cushion bomb. As the laughter reached its peak, Mark unleashed his arsenal. The rubber chicken soared through the air, and the whoopee cushion bomb exploded in a cacophony of flatulence.

Pandemonium erupted as Emperor Elon's laughter subsided. He looked around, bewildered by the chaos. Mark approached, holding a bouquet of exploding flowers.

"Your reign of laughter ends here, Elon!" Mark declared.

Elon, surprisingly composed despite the mayhem, responded in his best King Julian impression, "Oh, you think you can stop me, Mr. Bhangu? Well, let's dance off for the fate of the world!"

And so, a dance-off of epic proportions began. Elon's moonwalk was out of this world, but Mark countered with the "Funky Chicken" like no one had ever seen. As the world watched in suspense, the fate of humanity hung in the balance.

In the end, it was a tie. Emperor Elon and Mark Zuckerberg collapsed in laughter, realizing the absurdity of it all. Elon decided that maybe taking over the world wasn't such a great idea after all, and Mark agreed that a world ruled by laughter wasn't such a bad place.

Together, they formed the "Ministry of Merriment," dedicated to spreading joy and hilarity across the globe. Emperor Elon's corporations turned their attention to creating the world's largest collection of oversized rubber duckies and whoopee cushions.

And so, in this zany future reality, Earth was ruled by laughter, with Emperor Elon and Mark Zuckerberg leading the charge. The world had never been happier, and every day felt like a wacky adventure straight out of a cartoon.

In the aftermath of the GigaGiggle Gala, the Ministry of Merriment, under the joint leadership of Emperor Elon and Mark Zuckerberg, worked tirelessly to bring joy to every corner of the world. They introduced policies like "Mandatory Joke Hour" and "Tickle Tuesdays," where laughter was not only encouraged but legally required.

Emperor Elon redirected his vast resources into creating even more whimsical corporations. "Tesla's Laughmobiles" became the world's leading provider of electric vehicles that played comedy sketches instead of traditional engine noises. "Boring Chuckles" reimagined underground transportation with a network of pneumatic tubes that propelled passengers through tunnels filled with hilarious sound effects.

Meanwhile, Mark Zuckerberg and the Guardians of Giggles expanded their mission. They transformed their circus-tent headquarters into a global amusement park known as "GuardianLand." It featured roller coasters with loop-de-loops of laughter and bumper cars that told dad jokes with every collision. Visitors left with tears of joy in their eyes and a newfound appreciation for slapstick humor.

One day, as Emperor Elon and Mark were brainstorming their next grand venture, a peculiar visitor arrived. It was none other than Jeff Bezos, dressed as a clown and accompanied by a troupe of Amazonian jesters. He proposed a friendly competition between the Ministry of Merriment and his newly formed "Amazonian Amusement Army" to see who could bring more laughter to the world.

The competition was on, and it was a global sensation. Cities were transformed into whimsical wonderlands as the Ministry and the Amazonians engaged in epic prank battles, balloon animal showdowns, and pie-throwing contests. It was a laughter Olympics like no other.

As the competition reached its climax, Emperor Elon and Jeff Bezos found themselves in a slapstick showdown at the "Chuckling Colosseum." They engaged in a hilarious duel involving whoopee cushions, squirting flowers, and custard pies. The world watched in stitches as the two billionaire clowns went toe-to-toe.

In the end, the competition concluded with a tie. The world had never seen such an outpouring of mirth and silliness. As they shook hands,

Emperor Elon and Jeff Bezos realized that laughter was not a finite resource, and there was room for multiple champions of comedy.

Together, they founded the "United Nations of Humor" to promote laughter, fun, and joy worldwide. The world had entered a new era, where leaders were more concerned with punchlines than power plays. Laughter had become the universal language of unity.

And so, in this whimsical future reality, Earth was no longer threatened by tyranny but ruled by the hilarious harmony of humor. Emperor Elon, Mark Zuckerberg, and Jeff Bezos became the triumvirate of comedy, and the world laughed happily ever after.

As the United Nations of Humor continued to flourish, Emperor Elon, Mark Zuckerberg, and Jeff Bezos embarked on a globe-trotting comedy tour known as the "Three Jesters' World Chuckle-tour." They traveled in a colorful and whimsical hot air balloon adorned with oversized clown shoes and rainbow-colored streamers, spreading laughter to even the remotest corners of the Earth.

Their tour was a spectacle of epic proportions. In every city they visited, they hosted massive open-air comedy festivals. People from all walks of life gathered to enjoy stand-up comedy, improv shows, and side-splitting performances by the world's funniest clowns, jesters, and comedians.

Emperor Elon, in his King Julian persona, danced tirelessly to the delight of the crowds. Mark Zuckerberg, the master of comedic timing, showcased his impeccable whoopee cushion skills. And Jeff Bezos, the newly minted "Jester Jeff," surprised everyone with his surprisingly witty one-liners.

Their journey took them to places like the "Guffaw Gorges" in the Himalayas, where monks and yetis joined in the laughter. They made a pit stop at the "Roaring Rainforest" in the Amazon, where parrots mimicked jokes, and even the toucans tried their beak at stand-up.

In the heart of the Sahara Desert, they set up the "Desert Oasis of Delight," complete with an oasis of giggles and an all-camel comedy troupe. The laughter echoed across the dunes, attracting nomads from miles away.

As they traveled, they spread a message of unity, joy, and the power of laughter to bridge cultural divides. The world had never been more connected, as people from different backgrounds came together to share their favorite jokes and comedic traditions.

But their journey wasn't just about laughter; it was also about giving back. The trio used their wealth to build "Humor Hospitals" in underserved areas, where laughter was prescribed as the best medicine. Patients would watch hilarious performances, and the healing power of laughter worked wonders.

Eventually, the Three Jesters' World Chuckle-tour circled back to their headquarters at GuardianLand. The tour had been a roaring success, and the world was a happier, more united place because of it. The United Nations of Humor had achieved what no organization before had done— making laughter a force for good.

Emperor Elon, Mark Zuckerberg, and Jester Jeff stood together on a stage shaped like a giant banana peel, addressing the world with their final message. They declared that humor and laughter were the greatest weapons against darkness and despair, and they urged everyone to keep spreading the joy.

As the sun set over GuardianLand, the world watched in awe as a brilliant display of fireworks burst into the sky, forming a laughing emoji and signaling the beginning of a new era—one where laughter reigned supreme, and the world was a happier, more colorful place.

And so, in this whimsical future reality, Earth had transformed into a planet of mirth, ruled by the laughter of Emperor Elon, Mark Zuckerberg, and Jester Jeff. The world laughed, smiled, and lived happily ever after, proving that humor truly had the power to change the world for the better.

In the years that followed, the legacy of the United Nations of Humor continued to thrive, and laughter remained at the heart of global culture. New leaders emerged, each with their own unique comedic flair, and the world had become a never-ending festival of fun and frolic.

Emperor Elon, Mark Zuckerberg, and Jester Jeff remained close friends and ambassadors of humor. They were often invited to mediate international disputes through laughter, resolving conflicts with clever quips and hilarious skits rather than with force. World peace had never seemed more achievable.

Emperor Elon, with his characteristic whimsy, had created a new corporation called "TickleTech," specializing in laughter-inducing gadgets and gizmos. Their ticklish drones flew across the skies, spreading chuckles and giggles in their wake. Every home had a "TickleBot," a household assistant designed to tell jokes, perform magic tricks, and make even the grumpiest of days a bit brighter.

 Mark Zuckerberg's Guardians of Giggles had evolved into an international network of laughter advocates. They trained comedy troops, organized laughter flash mobs, and distributed "Giggle Guides" to communities around the world, encouraging the cultivation of humor as a way of life.

Jester Jeff's Amazonian Amusement Army, despite its competitive beginnings, had become a sister organization to the United Nations of Humor. They worked side by side to create laughter-themed events and humanitarian initiatives. Jester Jeff's corporation, "GigglePrime," was known for its philanthropic efforts, funding laughter therapy programs in hospitals and schools.

As the years rolled on, new challenges arose, but the world faced them with humor and optimism. Climate change was combated through "Comedy Carbon Credits," where individuals reduced their carbon footprint by making people laugh. Scientists developed "Giggle Green Energy," harnessing the power of laughter for sustainable electricity.

Even intergalactic diplomacy improved, with extraterrestrial civilizations visiting Earth and sharing in the universal language of comedy. Earth's first ambassador to the cosmos was none other than Emperor Elon, who proved that humor could bridge the vastness of space.

And so, in this utopian future, Earth was a planet of perpetual merriment, governed by a harmonious trio of laughter-loving leaders. People celebrated diversity, resolved conflicts with punchlines instead of punches, and remembered that a smile could be the most potent weapon against despair.

As the world continued to evolve, one thing remained constant: the sound of laughter, echoing from the streets of every city, the heart of every home, and the soul of every human being. In this world of endless hilarity and camaraderie, humanity thrived, for it had discovered that the most precious resource of all was not gold or power but the joyous laughter that bound them together.

In this world of perpetual laughter, humanity had reached new heights of creativity and innovation. With humor as the driving force, new inventions and industries flourished in ways never before imagined.

The Giggleverse

A new dimension of digital entertainment was born – the Giggleverse. Virtual reality worlds where people could immerse themselves in absurd, comical, and hilarious adventures. From bungee jumping off banana peels to solving riddles in a land of puns, these immersive experiences brought laughter to a whole new level.

The LaughTernet

The LaughTernet became the primary global communication platform. Instead of sending texts or emails, people communicated through jokes, comedic sketches, and humorous memes. Social media platforms like "TickleTalk" and "LaughBook" brought people together through laughter, making trolling a thing of the past.

The Ministry of Mirth

With Emperor Elon's leadership, the Ministry of Mirth expanded its efforts to provide humanitarian aid worldwide. They dispatched "Joy Jets" filled with laughter-inducing supplies to disaster-stricken areas, lifting spirits and aiding recovery efforts.

The Chuckle-cademy

Education took a playful turn with the establishment of the Chuckle-cademy. Traditional subjects were taught with a comedic twist, making learning fun for all ages. Students attended classes in oversized classrooms shaped like giant clown shoes.

The Galactic Gigglespace Alliance

Humanity's infectious sense of humor attracted the attention of neighboring planets. The Galactic Gigglespace Alliance was formed, where civilizations from across the cosmos came together to share laughter and trade their best jokes. Earth became a hub for intergalactic comedy festivals.

The Hilarious Health Movement

Thanks to the healing power of laughter, healthcare was revolutionized. "Comedy Clinics" offered laughter therapy sessions, and "Chuckling Yoga" became the go-to exercise for physical and mental well-being.

The Laugh to the Moon Initiative

With the help of SpaceX, Emperor Elon initiated the "Laugh to the Moon" program. Giant moon bases were established for lunar comedians to perform stand-up under Earth's night sky. It became a celestial comedy club, visible to all, and an inspiration for stargazers.

Despite the world's transformation into a comedy utopia, challenges still arose, but they were met with resilience and humor. The United Nations of Humor, now a coalition of laughter-loving leaders from around the world, worked tirelessly to address global issues with jokes and jests.

Even the most serious international negotiations were infused with humor, making diplomacy more effective and enjoyable. Conflicts were resolved through laughter battles, where opposing sides told jokes until everyone forgot why they were arguing in the first place.

In this world, laughter was more than a pastime; it was a way of life. People from every culture, background, and corner of the world came together in joyous harmony, embracing the belief that a good laugh could solve anything.

And so, Earth continued to spin in a state of perpetual mirth, a shining example of how humor, kindness, and unity could create a brighter future for all. As the world embraced the power of laughter, they discovered that the ultimate treasure was not gold or power, but the boundless capacity to bring joy to one another.

As the years rolled on in this world of boundless laughter and unity, there emerged a new generation of comedians, clowns, and jesters who were celebrated as heroes of the modern era. These laughter champions performed in grand arenas and coliseums, spreading joy with their witty banter, slapstick routines, and whimsical antics.

The Chuckle Olympics

Every four years, the Chuckle Olympics brought together the world's finest humorists to compete in laughter-inducing events. The Stand-up Sprint, the Puns and Giggles Relay, and the Slapstick High Dive were just a few of the side-splitting competitions that kept audiences in stitches.

The International Hug-a-thon

A global event where people from all walks of life came together to break the world record for the longest group hug. The event aimed to promote unity, empathy, and the healing power of human connection. It became a symbol of love and compassion.

The Laughalution

A movement that aimed to replace traditional New Year's Eve celebrations with global laugh-ins. People across the planet joined in a synchronized countdown to laughter, ushering in each new year with a burst of joy and hilarity.

The Museum of Merriment

A vast museum dedicated to the history of humor, showcasing everything from the first jesters of ancient civilizations to the iconic comedians of the 20th century. Visitors could step into interactive exhibits and even try their hand at creating their own jokes.

The Cosmic Comedy Festival

Earth's reputation for humor spread far beyond its borders. Extraterrestrial visitors flocked to the annual Cosmic Comedy Festival, where alien comedians joined their human counterparts in a galaxy-spanning celebration of laughter.

The Ministry of Laughter

The Ministry of Mirth evolved into the Ministry of Laughter, with a focus on promoting humor as a means to address serious global challenges. They organized "Laugh-Ins" at international summits, where world leaders were encouraged to share a joke before addressing critical issues.

Despite the lightheartedness that dominated Earth, the world faced occasional dilemmas. The United Nations of Humor worked in tandem with the Ministry of Laughter to resolve these challenges using their trademark humor and wit. Negotiations between nations often resembled comedy sketches, defusing tensions with punchlines instead of ultimatums.

In this world, laughter had become a universal currency. Acts of kindness and generosity were measured in chuckles, and compassion was the world's most sought-after commodity. It was a place where people of all backgrounds lived in harmony, where differences were celebrated with humor, and where the spirit of unity prevailed.

The legacy of Emperor Elon, Mark Zuckerberg, and Jester Jeff endured as a testament to the transformative power of laughter. Their vision of a world governed by joy had not only become a reality but had transcended expectations. It was a world where the greatest treasure was the gift of laughter itself, and everyone was a wealth of joy to share with others.

In this world of boundless laughter and camaraderie, Earth was a beacon of hope and merriment, drawing the attention of neighboring galaxies and distant civilizations. The laughter-loving inhabitants of the planet had unlocked the secret to universal harmony, and their influence reached far beyond their home world.

The Galactic Carnival

Earth became known as the Galactic Carnival, a destination for tourists from across the cosmos. Aliens traveled light-years to experience the unique blend of humor and unity that Earth had to offer. The intergalactic festival showcased performances from a multitude of species, each with their own brand of comedy.

The Global Guffaw Grid

An interconnected network of laughter-powered energy sources spanned the globe. Giant laugh reactors harnessed the collective chuckles and guffaws of humanity to generate clean, renewable energy. Earth had become a beacon of sustainability and hilarity.

The Peaceful Prankster Pact

Nations around the world formed the Peaceful Prankster Pact, a mutual agreement to resolve conflicts through elaborate pranks rather than war. Diplomatic tensions were defused with joyous practical jokes, and the art of the prank became a celebrated form of diplomacy.

The Holo-Humor Libraries

Libraries of the future were transformed into Holo-Humor Libraries, where holographic comedians and hologram-enhanced books provided endless entertainment and laughter. People could check out comedians like they checked out books, taking home a dose of humor for the soul.

The Time-Traveling Titters

Scientists discovered a way to harness laughter to power time machines. Travelers could now journey back in time to share jokes with historical figures, ensuring that laughter echoed through the ages and contributed to a happier past.

The Laughter Lagoon

Earth's oceans were transformed into "Laughter Lagoons," where marine life and humans alike enjoyed aquatic comedy shows. Dolphin stand-up comedians and clownfish jesters became the stars of the deep blue, bringing smiles to oceanic depths.

As Earth's reputation for humor and unity spread throughout the universe, extraterrestrial civilizations sought diplomatic relations and trade agreements based on laughter. The concept of interstellar comedy exchanges became the norm, fostering intergalactic cooperation and understanding.

The legacy of Emperor Elon, Mark Zuckerberg, and Jester Jeff continued to inspire future generations to embrace humor as a force for good. Their vision had not only transformed Earth but had rippled across the cosmos, making the universe a more joyful and interconnected place.

29

In this world, the laughter that bound humanity together had become the most valuable resource of all. It was a world where the joyous spirit of unity, compassion, and humor prevailed, reminding everyone that even in the face of challenges, a hearty laugh could heal wounds, bridge divides, and create a brighter future for all.